E READER MCK
McKay, Sindy
My car trip

Please check all items for damages
before leaving the Library.
Thereafter you will be held
responsible for all injuries
to items beyond reasonable wear.

Helen M. Plum Memorial Library

Lombard, Illinois

A daily fine will be charged for
overdue materials.

With fond memories of all my family vacations . . .

—D. P.

Parent's Introduction

We Both Read is the first series of books designed to invite parents and children to share the reading of a story by taking turns reading aloud. This "shared reading" innovation, which was developed with reading education specialists, invites parents to read the more complex text and storyline on the left-hand pages. Children can then be encouraged to read the right-hand pages, which feature less complex text and storyline, specifically written for the beginning reader. You will note that a "talking parent" icon ☺ precedes the parent's text and a "talking child" icon ☺ precedes the child's text.

Reading aloud is one of the most important activities parents can share with their child to assist them in their reading development. However, *We Both Read* goes beyond reading *to* a child and allows parents to share the reading *with* a child. *We Both Read* is so powerful and effective because it combines two key elements in learning: "modeling" (the parent reads) and "doing" (the child reads). The result is not only faster reading development for the child, but a much more enjoyable and enriching experience for both!

You may find it helpful to read the entire book aloud yourself the first time, then invite your child to participate in the second reading. We encourage you to share and interact with your child as you read the book together. If your child is having difficulty, you might want to mention a few things to help them. "Sounding out" is good, but it will not work with all words. They can pick up clues about the words they are reading from the story, the context of the sentence, or even the pictures. Some stories have rhyming patterns that might help. For beginning readers, you also might want to suggest touching the words with their finger as they read, so they can better connect the voice sound and the printed word.

Sharing the *We Both Read* books together will engage you and your child in an interactive adventure in reading! It is a fun and easy way to encourage and help your child to read—and a wonderful way to start them off on a lifetime of reading enjoyment!

We Both Read: My Car Trip

Text Copyright © 2005 by Sindy McKay
Illustrations Copyright ©2005 by Meredith Johnson
All rights reserved

We Both Read® is a trademark of Treasure Bay, Inc.

Published by Treasure Bay, Inc.
40 Sir Francis Drake Boulevard
San Anselmo, CA 94960 USA

PRINTED IN SINGAPORE

Library of Congress Catalog Card Number: 2004115435
Hardcover ISBN: 1-891327-63-1
Paperback ISBN: 1-891327-64-X

05 06 07 08 09 / 10 9 8 7 6 5 4 3 2 1

We Both Read® Books
Patent No. 5,957,693

Visit us online at:
www.webothread.com

WE BOTH READ®

My Car Trip

By Sindy McKay

Illustrated by Meredith Johnson

TREASURE BAY

We're taking a car trip. We're traveling far.

We're visiting Grandpa. We're driving the . . .

. . . car.

I love it at Grandpa's. It's never a bore.

He lives in the country and runs his own . . .

. . . store.

"Let's go!" calls my father. "We're all loaded up!"

I buckle my seat belt and so does my . . .

. . . pup.

My dad tells my mom she's in charge of the map. Then he turns on the engine and puts on his . . .

. . . cap.

We head for the highway, but then we **get stuck**.
Up ahead on the road is a broken **down** . . .

. . . truck.

We finally move and it's nice for a bit.

But all you can do is watch scenery and . . .

. . . sit.

I'm getting so bored! And the trip is so long!

Then Mom turns and says to me, "Let's sing . . .

. . . a song."

My mom knows a song that goes, "Are we there yet?"
My dad knows a song about flying . . .

. . . a jet.

The singing is fun and it helps the time pass.

Before we all know it, it's time to get . . .

. . . gas.

Then Dad says, "Who's hungry?" and I shout out, "Me!"
We drive to a café and park by . . .

. . . a tree.

I order a burger and big batch of fries.

Then I choose my dessert from a big tray of . . .

. . . pies.

My dog waits so patiently 'til we're all done.

I put on his leash and we go for . . .

. . . a run.

I take my dog back and he climbs in my lap.

While Dad keeps on driving, we both take . . .

. . . a nap.

I dream about Grandpa, just waiting for me.

I dream of his store and the cool things I'll . . .

. . . see.

Inside of his store there are fish poles and pails.

And lanterns and cook stoves and hammers . . .

. . . and nails.

There's dish soap and tissues and puzzles with words.

There's popcorn and apples and seed for . . .

. . . the birds.

There's even a rocking chair and an old trunk.
And stuff to wash up in, if you meet . . .

. . . a skunk.

My mom wakes me up and says, "Honey, we're here."
I look out the window and see a few . . .

. . . deer.

We pull up the driveway and now I can see,
that Grandpa is outside, just waiting for . . .

. . . me.

We've travelled all day and we're finally done.
The car trip was long, but it really was . . .

. . . fun.

If you liked *My Car Trip*, here are two other We Both Read® Books you are sure to enjoy!

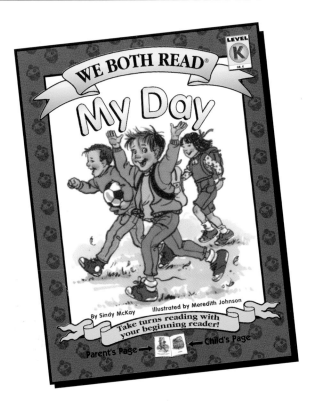

This Level K book is designed for the child who is just being introduced to reading. The child's pages have only one or two words, which relate directly to the illustration and even rhyme with what has just been read to them. This title is a charming story about what a child does in the course of a simple happy day.

To see all the We Both Read books that are available,
just go online to **www.webothread.com**

Suzu has asked for a white cat for her birthday. Now,
on the night before her birthday, she begins to find
cats all over the house—most of them in very unusual
colors! Suzu loves cats, but now she has too many!
Focusing on reading the names for colors and the
numbers from one to ten, this book is designed for
the child who is just being introduced to reading.